To my parents who have always loved and supported me
DM

To my incredible children who continually fill my life with blessings
SJB

Frog Has No Fur

FREE MUSIC
thelittlefig.com

La Rana No Tiene Pelo

So Big & Little Bit Adventures™
Creators S. J. Bushue & Deb McQueen

Published by the little fig, LLC

I am called So Big.

Me llaman Tan Grande.

I am called Little Bit.

Me llaman Pequeñito.

We are best friends!

¡Somos los mejores amigos!

Why are you friends?
You are not alike!

¿Por qué son amigos?
¡Ustedes no son parecidos!

Oh my!
We are NOT alike!

¡Caramba! ¡NO somos parecidos!

I am big and brown.

Soy grande y marrón.

I am little and green.

Soy pequeño y verde.

I have fur.

Tengo pelo.

I am a mammal.

Yo soy mamífero.

I am an amphibian.

Yo soy anfibio.

I live on land and in water.

Yo vivo en la tierra y en el agua.

I hunt for food in the day

Yo cazo para la comida por el día

and sleep at night.

y duermo por la noche.

I hide in the day

Me escondo por el día

and hunt at night.

y cazo por la noche.

My heart has
4 chambers.

Mi corazón tiene 4 cámaras.

My heart has
3 chambers.

Mi corazón tiene 3 cámaras.

I have ears.

Tengo orejas.

My whole eye turns.
I see you!

Todo mi ojo gira. ¡Te veo!

First to walk on land!

¡El primero a caminar sobre la tierra!

I made it 100 million years later.

Lo hice 100 millones de años después.

We do not have to be the same.
We are friends...

No tenemos que ser el mismo. Somos amigos....

... just because we like each other.

.... sólo porque nos gustamos.

Can we be your friends too?

¿Podemos ser tus amigos también?

Text copyright © 2013 by S. J. Bushue
Illustrations copyright © 2014 by Debra McQueen

Special thanks to Marlee Coyne, Megan Dieme', Robin & Blake Hicks, George Hunt,
and Alex & Jennifer Smith

All inquiries should be addressed to:
The Little Fig, LLC™
P.O. Box 26073, Overland Park, KS 66225 USA
www.thelittlefig.com
Printed in USA

So Big & Little Bit Adventures™ are trademarks of The Little Fig, LLC™

Second Edition, February 2015
Library of Congress Control Number: 2014910883

ISBN-13   978-1-63333-011-5